JESTINE
NEEDS TO CLEAN

By a.d. storm

Interior Art Credit: Brian Mumphrey

Archway Publishing books may be ordered through booksellers or by contacting:

Archway Publishing
1663 Liberty Drive
Bloomington, IN 47403
www.archwaypublishing.com
1 (888) 242-5904

ISBN: 978-1-4808-5903-6 (sc)
ISBN: 978-1-4808-5901-2 (hc)
ISBN: 978-1-4808-5902-9 (e)

Print information available on the last page.

Archway Publishing rev. date: 02/26/2018

For William & Jestine

Dedicated to my mother Pauline

Special thanks to:
Dianne Evans, Mary LaBarbera,
Rhonda Silver, Baba Storm, Verna Tweddale

Other titles by a.d. storm:
Dottie Doo and Pepper Roo Do Something New

This is Jestine.

She needs to clean.

She found some old cheese that had turned a weird green.

Jestine really knew, that she needed to clean.

She counted the ants on it,
and there were nineteen.

Jestine really knew, that
she needed to clean.

Her messes were many, and they made quite a gross scene.

Jestine really knew, that she needed to clean.

She found a damp blob,
that looked like a spleen.

Jestine really knew, that
she needed to clean.

She slipped on an orange,
that had turned aquamarine.

Jestine really knew, that
she needed to clean.

She looked 'round at the worst filth that she'd ever seen.

And Jestine really saw, that she needed to clean.

She wiped and she washed
'til there was a nice sheen.

And Jestine liked things better,
when they were clean.

She went up, down and sideways, and all in between.

Jestine was starting to enjoy being clean.

She found an old toy, she had named "Mr. Mc Bean".

Jestine loved what she found, when she started to clean!

She even pretended to be,
a dirt-seeking machine.

Jestine could have fun,
when she started to clean.

She even straightened her tree,
which had started to lean.

Jestine was so glad that
she had started to clean.

When the job was all done, everything was pristine.

Jestine was so proud, and downright serene.